THIS **Elephant & Piggie** BOOK
BELONGS TO:

_____

_____

_____

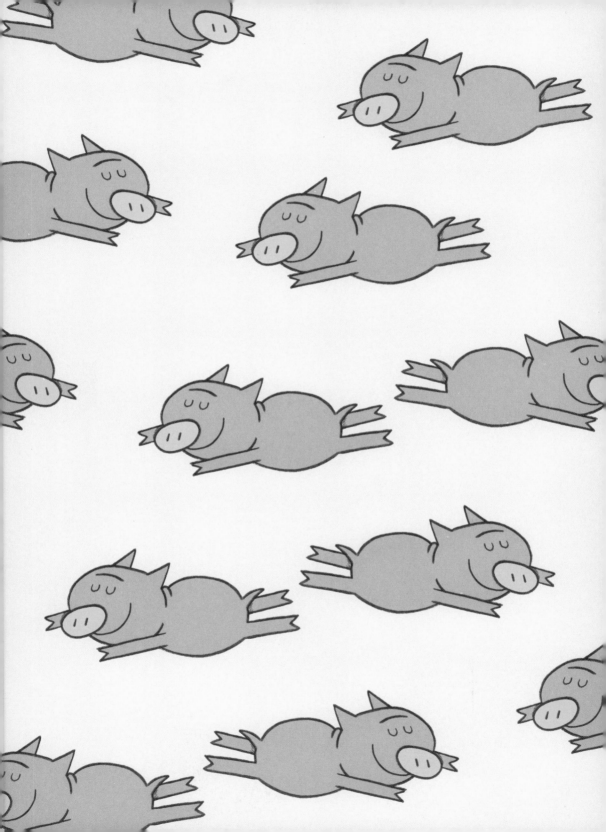

To my friend Alessandra

Today I Will Fly!

Mo Willems

WALKER BOOKS
AND SUBSIDIARIES
LONDON • BOSTON • SYDNEY • AUCKLAND

An Elephant & Piggie Book

Today I will fly!

You will not fly tomorrow.

You will not fly
next week.

9

Goodbye.

She will not fly.

Fly, fly, fly, fly, fly

fly, fly, fly, fly, fly!

Fly, fly, fly, fly!

You need help.

I will get help!

You did *not* fly.

I jumped?

Yes, it was a big jump.
But you did not fly.

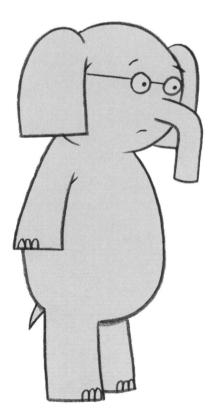

I will try again!

I will eat lunch.

Goodbye!

Fly! Fly! Fly!

I do need help.

Will you help me?

I will.
I will help you.

Thank you.

Hello?

Hello!

You are flying today!

I am *not* flying!

50

I am getting help.

Tomorrow *I* will fly!

Mo Willems is the renowned author of many award-winning books,
including the Caldecott Honor winners *Don't Let the Pigeon Drive the Bus!*,
Knuffle Bunny and *Knuffle Bunny Too*. His other groundbreaking picture books
include *Knuffle Bunny Free*, *Leonardo, the Terrible Monster* and *Edwina:
The Dinosaur Who Didn't Know She Was Extinct*. Before making picture books,
Mo was a writer and animator on Sesame Street, where he won six Emmys.
Mo lives with his family in Massachusetts, USA.

Visit him online at **www.mowillems.com** and **www.GoMo.net**

This is a work of fiction. Names, characters, places and incidents are either
the product of the author's imagination or, if real, used fictitiously.

First published in Great Britain 2008 by Walker Books Ltd
87 Vauxhall Walk, London SE11 5HJ

First published in the United States by Hyperion Books for Children
British publication rights arranged with Sheldon Fogelman Agency, Inc.

This edition published 2012

8 10 9 7

© 2007, 2012 Mo Willems

The right of Mo Willems to be identified as author and illustrator of this work has been
asserted by him in accordance with the Copyright, Designs and Patents Act 1988

This book has been typeset in Century 725 and Grilled Cheese

Printed in China

British Library Cataloguing in Publication Data:
a catalogue record for this book is available from the British Library

ISBN 978-1-4063-3848-5

www.walker.co.uk